# My SCHOOLHOUSE Rocks!

Written by Katlynne Mirabal · Illustrated by Timerie Blair

I can stay in pajamas with momma all day.

I can build pillowforts    to hide in and play.

I can jump in big puddles on days that it rains.

My schoolhouse rocks!

I can count in Spanish as I sit on the stairs.

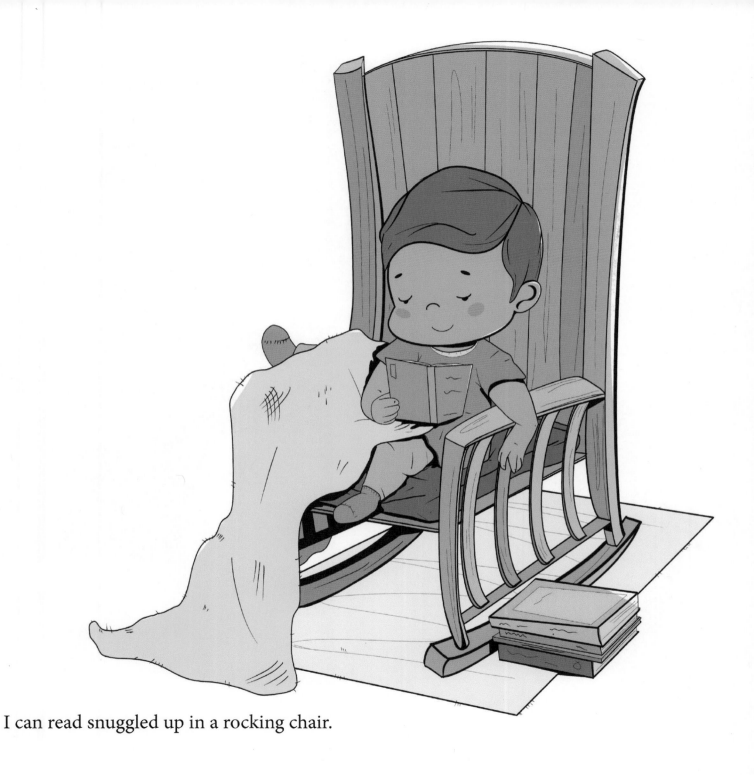

I can read snuggled up in a rocking chair.

I can play piano in my underwear.

My schoolhouse rocks!

I can feed the dog in a t-shirt and socks.

I can practice writing with colorful chalk.

I can hunt for bugs on our morning walk.

My schoolhouse rocks!

I can bake yummy cookies while practicing math.

I can recite poems in the bubble bath.

I can paint funny pictures that make me laugh.

My schoolhouse rocks.

I can explore outer space  and chew bubblegum.

I can harvest our garden with my green thumb.

I can hunt down ancestors to see where I'm from.

My schoolhouse rocks!

When the moon shines bright, I hop into bed.

Dad reads me a story and kisses my head.

I can't wait for tomorrow to do it again.